Farmer Kobi's Hanukkah Match

by Karen Rostoker-Gruber and Rabbi Ron Isaacs
illustrations by CB Decker

Springfield, NJ • Jerusalem

This fictional story is dedicated to my cousin Yehuda Shlain, who was born on the famous Nahalal Moshav, founded in 1921. Also a HUGE thank-you to my uncle Willie Rostoker, and my cousins Ronit Rostoker, Orly Bloomenfeld, and Shachar Shlain for answering all of my crazy questions and photographic requests. I wouldn't have been able to work on this book without you.
—K.R-G

This book is dedicated to Zach and Courtney.
—R.H.I

To Matt and Kyle . . . there's a lesson here somewhere.
—C.B.D.

Apples & Honey Press
An imprint of Behrman House and Gefen Publishing House
Behrman House, 11 Edison Place, Springfield, New Jersey 07081
Gefen Publishing House Ltd., 6 Hatzvi Street, Jerusalem 94386, Israel
www.applesandhoneypress.com

Text copyright © 2015 KRG Entertainment, LLC
A note for families copyright © 2015 Rabbi Ron Isaacs
Illustrations copyright © 2015 Behrman House Inc.
Edited by Ann Koffsky and Dena Neusner

ISBN 978-1-68115-501-2

Library of Congress Cataloging-in-Publication Data
Rostoker-Gruber, Karen.
Farmer Kobi's Hanukkah match / by Karen Rostoker-Gruber and Rabbi Ron Isaacs ;
illustrations by CB Decker.
pages cm
Summary: On the second night of Hanukkah, Farmer Kobi invites Polly to his home for dinner but her reaction to his animals proves she is not his perfect match, while a stranger who appears at the door just might be. Includes a note about Jewish values and how the story can be used to teach them to one's children.
ISBN 978-1-68115-501-2 (hardcover) [1. Dating (Social customs)—Fiction. 2. Human-animal relationships—Fiction. 3. Domestic animals—Fiction. 4. Farm life—Fiction.
5. Jews—Fiction. 6. Hanukkah—Fiction. 7. Humorous stories.] I. Isaacs, Ronald H. II. Decker, C. B., illustrator. III. Title.
PZ7.R72375Far 2015   [E]--dc23   2014027243
Design by David Neuhaus/NeuStudio
Printed in China
1 3 5 7 9 8 6 4 2

Donkey's legs shook so hard he could barely stand. Tonight, on the second night of Hanukkah, Farmer Kobi had invited Polly to his farm for a date. Donkey wanted the date to go smoothly.

Farmer Kobi had the biggest
farm on the moshav and had lots of
animal friends. But he wanted a human
friend, one who would be his perfect match.
Farmer Kobi thought his perfect match might be Polly.
She seemed kind-hearted. Donkey hoped so.

"Polly will be here in *eggz–actly* five minutes," honked the geese. "What's taking Farmer Kobi so long? We've already polished the menorah."

"And we've put out the candles, dreidels, and *gelt*," maaed the goats.

"*Bleats* us," baaed the sheep. "His food is warming up and the *baa-baa ghanoush* is already done."

"Let's see if he needs any help," hee-hawed Donkey.

The geese, goats, and sheep followed Donkey to Farmer Kobi's room. "I don't know what to wear."

The geese went into his closet. "You'd look nice in this *eggshell*–white shirt."

"With these *blaaack* pants," maaed the goats.

"With this *maaaroon* wool sweater," baaed the sheep.

Farmer Kobi put everything on and looked in the mirror.
"What do you think?"

"Hee-haw-wow!" said Donkey.

"You look *flap-ulous*," honked the geese.

"Just *maaa-velous*," maaed the goats.

"*Aaab-solutely* striking!" baaed the sheep.

Knock, knock!

Farmer Kobi answered the door. The animals were right behind him.

"Happy Hanukkah, Polly."

"Thank you, Kobi."

"Come on in and sit down," said Farmer Kobi. "Wait until you see what I've cooked up for us tonight."

"I could get used to this," said Polly.

The geese took her hat. The goats took her coat. The sheep pulled out a chair for her. Donkey nudged her in.

"Oh my," giggled Polly. "Shouldn't your animals be outside?"

"I wanted them to meet you."

"Charmed," Polly mumbled.

"I smell something burning," said Farmer Kobi. "I'll be right back."

The geese brought Polly a Hanukkah song sheet.

"Don't expect me to sing to you," whispered Polly. "Shouldn't you animals be outside chasing things?"

The sheep brought Polly the *shamash* and menorah.

"I didn't come here to light the menorah with animals," snapped Polly. "Shoo, shoo!"

Farmer Kobi came back from the kitchen carrying baba ghanoush.

"Mmmmm. That smells wonderful, Kobi."

"Wait until you see what else I've cooked," said Farmer Kobi, as he went back to get another dish.

Donkey folded Polly's napkin.

The geese poured her limonana.

The goats gave Polly gelt and a dreidel.

"Don't expect me to play dreidel with a bunch of animals," whispered Polly. "Get out of here!"

She opened the door to let the animals out. NOT ONE animal budged.

Farmer Kobi came back
carrying falafel.
"Are the animals bothering you?"
"Oh, not at all," Polly said sweetly.
Farmer Kobi went to get
another dish.

"I hope the next dish is lamb chops topped with goose pâté," she whispered to the animals.

The goats filled her plate with falafel.

"Get away from me!" hissed Polly quietly.

"Is everything okay over there?" called Farmer Kobi.

"Just spiffy," answered Polly.

Farmer Kobi carried in potato latkes with homemade applesauce and sour cream.

"Kobi, I thought we were going to be alone tonight," Polly whispered.

"They don't mean any harm," said Farmer Kobi. "They're just trying to get to know you."

"Getting to know me?! There are feathers floating in my limonana, drool on the dreidel, wool wound 'round the menorah, and mud mushed into my dress. I came here to get to know you better, not them. If I wanted to be with animals, I'd go to the zoo!"

Slam!

Farmer Kobi stared at the door.

The animals didn't know what to do. The food was getting cold.

"She was definitely NOT Farmer Kobi's perfect *maaatch*," maaed the goats.

"Her name was *Polly Ester*—she was a *faaake*," baaed the sheep.

"She was one rotten egg," honked the geese.

Knock, knock!

"Maybe it's Polly," maaed the goats. "*Maaagically* returning to apologize."

Donkey answered the door. It wasn't Polly. It was a lady with a friendly smile.

"Hi. My name is Ruthie. I hate to bother you, but I have a flat tire. May I use your phone?"

Farmer Kobi stared at her.

"Oh, I'm sorry," said Ruthie. "It looks like you were just about to celebrate."

The geese brought her the phone.

"Oh, what smart geese!"

The goats took her coat.

"What adorable goats!"

The sheep pulled out a chair for her.

"What a lovely family."

Donkey carried over a fork and a small bowl filled with baba ghanoush for her to taste. "Mmmmm. That's sooooo good."

"You must be hungry," said Farmer Kobi. "Would you like to join us for dinner and a game of dreidel?"

"I'd love to, but my family is waiting for me in the truck."

"Invite them in," said Farmer Kobi.

"We have more than enough."

Donkey looked at Ruthie's truck.
"Hee–haw–yahoo!" said Donkey.
Ruthie was Farmer Kobi's perfect match.

Words to Know

Moshav A cooperative farming community in Israel.

Limonana A popular Israeli drink that combines lemonade and mint leaves.

Shamash The candle that is used to light the other candles.

Baba ghanoush A spicy dish made with mashed eggplant and olive oil.

Falafel Deep-fried chickpea balls.

A Note for Families

Sharing the story of Farmer Kobi can be a wonderful way to start a discussion on Jewish values with your child.

Compassion for Animals: Tza'ar Ba'alei Chayyim

Jewish tradition shows great concern for the welfare of animals. Animals are included in the commandment to rest on Shabbat, and the ancient rabbis advised people to feed their animals before eating their own meals. After sharing the story of Farmer Kobi and his animals, talk with your child about the following related ideas:

Do you think that Farmer Kobi is kind to animals? Is Polly? Is Ruthie?

Why is it important to be kind to animals?

Welcoming Guests: Hachnasat Orchim

Welcoming guests is one of the most pleasant commandments to perform. The Torah describes how our ancestors Abraham and Sarah rushed to bring refreshments to their guests, and the rabbinic sage Rabbi Huna would stand outside his door and announce, "Let all who are hungry come in to eat." After reading about Farmer Kobi hosting guests, invite your child to think about the following questions:

Were Farmer Kobi's animals good hosts?

What did they do to make Polly and Ruthie feel welcome?

What actions can you take to help guests feel comfortable in your home?